Dora Stuart Menteath

Avalon

A Poetic Romance

Dora Stuart Menteath

Avalon
A Poetic Romance

ISBN/EAN: 9783337049256

Printed in Europe, USA, Canada, Australia, Japan

Cover: Foto ©Andreas Hilbeck / pixelio.de

More available books at **www.hansebooks.com**

AVALON

AVALON:

A POETIC ROMANCE.

BY

DORA STUART-MENTEATH.

———

𝕷𝖔𝖓𝖉𝖔𝖓 :

JAMES ELLIOTT AND CO.,

TEMPLE CHAMBERS, FALCON COURT,

FLEET STREET, E.C.

——

1894.

G

THE ARGUMENT.

LABAN MORDRED, *representing the ambition which is of earth and the achievement which is of earth, seeks and believes himself to attain at length the great Catholicon, the elixir of immortal life. Here is material ambition at its highest, science in the material order at the apex of achievement, but it is baffled even in the attainment of the Supreme Secret. Here also is reason perishing on the threshold of the Grand Mystery. By the side of this earthly ambition, and in one sense the daughter thereof, is spiritual aspiration, seeking the Holy Grail, the ideal of humanity, and the perfect order. Angela is not of earth, and yet is she the child of earth; she has another and truer home, and an inheritance in the Great Mystery. Here is the sublimed efflorescence of purified desire; here is that which accompanies and shares the pilgrimage of earthly humanity, the daughter of reason, but differing from reason—it is the Soul. She is also the higher womanhood in search of the higher manhood, typified by Arthur. Arthur in one aspect represents the archetypal man, the divine pattern from which the race has deflected, and in this sense he is not wounded, but in another he is the inner greatness of humanity which is wounded by the imperfection of mankind. Under either aspect he is now withdrawn and unmanifest, abiding in restful, spiritual Avalon, the world of the within. The love of Angela for the hidden King is the desire of Psyche after Pneuma. The Holy Grail is the divine principle of healing, by which man is made whole. And this can be love alone, but it is love spiritualised, elevated, and directed to perfection. So is the gift sought without by Angela in reality to be found within, whence she attains it in vision only, or otherwise in the inner world. And the true manhood, the archetype, the divine pattern is within also, and so Arthur is likewise reached in vision. But these things, if they are to profit man, must be manifested outwardly in humanity, divine love must return to earth for the exaltation of the race, and hence in the final vision, under the ministry of the Holy Grail, the face of the King is manifested as the face of*

Paul, the earthly lover of Angela. So is spiritual love brought into the service of man, and the natural desire of earth unified with higher desire begins to actualize here and now the sublime enthusiasm of the ideal.

AVALON.

A ROMANCE.

PROEM.

DESCEND in silence, and the world
    restore,

Dew of the evening—from thy crystal
    height

Fall, clarify, and cleanse! In lane and
    hedge

Awaken'd perfume breathes. And thou,
    cool mist,

Subdue the flaming splendours of the sky,

And modulate the glare of passing day

To the rich twilight of the dreamful tone,

Which leaves a holy space for haunting
    thought

B

'Twixt eve and night, when lambent
    vesper shews
A broken beam ; when the soft wind is
    hush'd
To tender breathings, and the life of
    earth,
Held in the balance of the gloaming time,
Soothes down to quiet music. Till the
    moon
Lifts up, belated in the clouded East,
The angry wonder of an orange arc,
And all the mist, dissolving, leaves the
    vault
Of purple heaven unveil'd from pole to
    pole ;
While in the glory of the northern stars,
Through night's whole length, there
    dwells a lasting sign
And certain promise of the day to come ;
Swathed by phantasmal mystery and
    doubt,

Some dreams may manifest a moment's
 space

Where all is spectral, and will scarce
 betray

Their ghostly vesture. In such eerie
 dusk

Alone the mind immersed will muse on
 thee,

Ghost-haunted, melancholy, far withdrawn,

O Avalon! For that brief mystic space

Beholding thee, will deem thy fable true,

Pass to the valley which thy silent sea

Has ring'd with magic, and have commune there

With the antique, subdued, and patient
 shades

That wait therein; but when the moon is
 high

The spell dissolves, and the wind, rising,
 sweeps

The last pale vestige past.   Perchance a
    few,
Appraising life as something less than
    dream,
And holding that the true and only life
Is that which men call dream, illumined
    souls,
May know the secret which prolongs
    such spells,
And Avalon for them is dream indeed ;
True dream, deep dream.

                        A dream of Avalon !
Green isle of apples, from the world
    apart,
Who enters thee, and on the savour
    sweet—
The next-world savour—of thy hidden
    fruit
Pastures his soul, from him the earth-
    curse falls,

Wrought first in the earth-mother of us
all.

Is Enoch waiting there, who walk'd with
God?

And rapt Elias, in the flaming car

Past ocean's utmost bounds withdrawn in
light—

Does he, too, wait, as golden legends tell,

In the hush'd temples of thy bowers
remote?

Do their eyes' dark light fill thy mystic
dales,

Thy placid rivers, thy diffusive founts,

Thy sprinkling sprigs of ballad melody,

With the rich soul, the dim, mysterious
soul

Of prophecy?—Where art thou—where?
Beyond

The Cornish wilds, the mountain, and the
mere,

Beyond the riot of the raving sea,

Spume-scatt'ring plumes and crumbling
    crests of waves

Crying in bitter madness, far beyond,

In some enchanted zone, a moving isle,

As seafolk tell, hast thou one place of
    rest—

The unknown centre of the western main?

O utmost island of this lower earth,

Art thou bedew'd indeed by Lethe's
    fount,

Or art thou Paradise and Aden ring'd

By the edged billows of the acrid sea

As by angelic swords, and hiding there

The crystal stairway of the starry world?

The elder legends name thee Isle of
    Saints,

The Bardic Land, of inspiration home.

Where thou art, there is peace ; but
    where art thou?

Near as the lips of lovers when they
    meet,

For close are all things beautiful and
    true :
Hard by our lives as is the gracious time
And Christ's good day.

The present in the past
Is merged for ever, and in turn sucks
    down
The future hour, and no dividing line
Subsists between them, for the three
    make up
Duration's phases, being one in three :
And when the ferment and the seething
    flow
Have settled into stillness, time assumes
The perfect mode, which is Eternity ;
And so between eternity and time
There is no greater cleavage than
    between
The bay's smooth water and the waves
    beyond ;

Through both the ebbing and the rising
  tide
Pass and repass.   Thou also, Avalon,
Art not a Sabbath journey's space from
  home ;
And if the life of man seem far from
  thee,
It is not distance, as of main or land,
Which   intervenes :   some   other   bar
  obstructs,
Some opposition in the state of life,
Whereof the tempest's tumult and fierce
  stress
Comport but little with thy grace serene,
And thy dream's solemnuess.

    Who wills may then
Most surely win thy wonder, to a type
Of softer life constrain that crusted mode
Which now we wear ; and he shall meet
  in thee

She cross'd the corridors ; the house was
  still

As deep sleep dreaming at the gate of
  death,

Or some hush'd watcher at the altar
  steps

When, 'twixt the mystery of night and
  morn,

The last red ray of the expending
  lamp

Casts its tinged light upon the silken
  veil

Which hides the mystery of life and
  peace.

And all the breathing sweetness of her
  life

Sank into stillness with a sudden chill

When the soft knocking of her gentle
  hand

Call'd forth no answer from the
  Alchemist.

That is stony cold

Which touches her; it is all over—all

Solved suddenly—do nothing: it is done

And finish'd, and whatever is beyond,

For act or thought, has settled evermore

To bitter unimportance. Ah, let be!

And let the dead arms take her, too,
to death,

And welcome void of death to void of
life;

So let her die, and raise from thy dim
world,

Spirit of dream, some other maid than
this

To take the task which thus will slip
from her—

The quest and healing of the King to
come;

Or otherwise God compass His great
ends;

Many a mile

Along the seaboard where the warlocks
  dwelt

In those old evil days by God wiped
  out—

Where now a peaceful colony abode

Bright as the smile sunning a gentle face

When gentle hands have wiped its tears
  away—

And many a mile along the country side—

Had pass'd the praise of Angela; the
  maids

And matrons, with the young men and
  the old,

As if the one heart of a strong, true
  man,

Loved her with something of the far-off
  love

Whereby the tide-wave on the open sea

Might yearn towards fair shores sphered
  in distant zones.

And she loved all after the angels' mode,

And shone on them as stars upon the
sea

From the unconscious height of heavenly
thought.

Yet pass'd she oft among the villagers,

Mild grace diffusing, happy influence,

The perfect courtesy and charm of
Christ;

And, though the former wealth of Mordred House

Had turn'd to ashes in the crucible,

Some surplus still remain'd from daily
needs

For her sweet charity's dispensing hand,

And comfort of the needy and the sick.

But far away from other tower or hall

The old hill-house lorded the land alone,

And few came thither of her own degree.

Yet some would come to woo her, whom
report

Had drawn from distant places up and
down
The Cornish land, because her beauty's
fame
Had spread through all the country of the
West;
And they went back who would have
woo'd a maid
And found an angel, worshipping went
back,
And evermore the house upon the hill
Was holy ground.

The alchemist, high up,
Within his smoke-dried chamber, wrought
in pain,
Passing all matters through his crucible,
And saw reluctant Nature one by one
Give up her guarded secrets to his gaze,
And aye the pure flame of his daughter's
prayers

Went on in hope before his daring
    quest,

She holding somehow that its end attain'd

Should help her own. So all her heart
    flow'd out

To Arthur daily, and her dreams at night

Beheld the blessed advent of the King,

Great Arthur on the throne of all the
    world,

And she that loved him somewhere at his
    feet

Accorded place, and dwelling in his light.

O Angela, sweet maiden Angela,

Blithe one and bright one, near us, dear
    to us,

Type of our soul, seek the great type
    of us !

Go thou to Arthur ! Lets not in thee,
    most pure,

That which lets in us. Avalon, Avalon—

Call we in vain thereon,—thou shalt go
    in !

'Tis not far travelling, here at thy hand—

Oh, not one space beyond thy floral
    bower !—

It is within thee ; through thy window's
    eyes

A poet lover, if his heart be clean,

Might look directly in its sweet recess.

Thou shalt bring Arthur out to us, out
    to us ;

So shall he rule us till we grow to him ;

When we have grown to him, in the ripe
    time,

Then shall he offer us perfect to Christ.

Pass on, pale Alchemist, iu peace pass
    on !

Up to thine utmost light thou hast well
    toil'd,

The demiourgos of the world that is,

Shaping the substance put into thy
    hands,
Digesting, sublimating, cocting all,
The separation of impure and pure
Effecting, latent virtue out of all
Evolving, and through all and all and all
Seeking the grand Quintessence. Thou
    hast fail'd;
Thy crucible has burst, thy fires are out,
The dust has gather'd on thine open
    scrolls,—
Here is an end to thy long processes.
Thou wast a patient searcher, well
    equipp'd
To question Nature and response wring
    out.
Thou hast transmuted, tinctured, modified,
No form eluded thine analysis.
But the great master Alchemist of death,
The all-transmuter, having need of thee,
Dissolves thee now into thine elements;

G

His simple process in a moment's time

Has stultified thy life-time of research.

O not within the metal or the mine

The secret lies !   Earth and the things of
    earth—

These do not hold it or their elements.

'Tis in the soul alone !   Science breaks
    down,

And reason, impotent to cross the bar,

Stands in the night and struggles with
    the veil,

Which seems to shift before the lightest
    touch,

Yet never reason rends or raises it.

Flash thy torch round it, thou strong
    faculty !

What seems that Titan shape in the
    blurr'd light ?

The silent sphinx with its eternal smile.

Long has it ceased to question or
    reply ;

Waste not thy breath with riddles !
    Hark, beyond
That is the blind wind beating through
    the gulf
Which roars and roars !

BOOK III.

THE FINDING OF THE GRAIL.

———

THE maid has wrestled with her
agony,
Died like a daughter in her father's
death—
Precipitated from the height of doom
In one fell moment on her daughter's
love—
And by the cup of immortality
Snatch'd from her lips, has died a second
time,
Repulsed from peaks of the eternal stars
Back to the level of mortality.
Now from this double draught of acrid
death,
And the long wasting of the woe within,

She brings a pallid fortitude at first

To face the future time, the ashes grey

Of dream and vision, and a sire's white
    shroud.

But soon the soul asserts itself within,

For Arthur lives, despite his grievous
    wound,

And Laban Mordred, alchemist, despite

Elixir spilt and shatter'd crucible,

Lives somewhere in the shadow of God's
    wings.

What, then, is immortality of earth?

What any heritage of earthly wealth?

Let it dissolve and die, so the soul
    live,

And come the King, sure master of the
    soul,

Till Christ come, who is master of the
    King.

And, more than all, come time, which
    time is not,

When Christ and King into the Father's
hands

Shall give the kingdom and the keys
thereof,

And all things shall dissolve and rest
with God;

When that without shall be as that
within,

And this poor life of self shall wholly
end.

So is she lighted by her suffering,

And, further taken from the things of
flesh,

The loving quest regards with alter'd
eye—

Sees midst what mountains broods the
Holy Grail,

Sees o'er what waters shineth Avalon—

Sees—chosen maiden, may we look with
thee!—

And, lo, the woe is past! Peace comes,
and light.
So from the highest hopes of earthly life,
Which in the ruddy tincture of the wise—
The healing draught that makes men
laugh at death
And unto leprous metals can impart
Gold's perfect form—have culminated,
she
Goes forth; from poetry and pure
romance—
An argent world, by dainty fancy
bless'd—
To seek the exaltation of the soul
She passes on, in her white light array'd,
The samite raiment of her maidenhood;
And henceforth ideality is hers.
Pass, holy vestal, pass from Mordred
House!
Pass, Angela, to find the Perfect Man,
And manifest a saviour to the age!

So from us also pass all earthly hopes,

So be we free to seek the grand and
  true!

Pass cold mistrust, the hoar-frost of the
  heart,

Pass selfish ends, and let us also go

Straight through the open portal of the
  flesh

Into the world of mind!

                    The perfect man

Perchance abode on the beloved earth

All in the pearl and rainbow morning
  time,

Master of light, ideal leader, lord;

Splendour and pomp of mind invested
  him,

True prince of this world and the powers
  thereof,

Not the poor fallen Lucifer who spreads

O'er earth this day his melancholy reign,

But the Great King, the morning star,
the King,

The bright, white King. O'er whom in
evil time

Prevail'd the fractious commerce of mis-
rule,

And now the perfect man has gone
from earth,

Who kept the baser part in holy thrall,

For man has sinn'd against the perfect
state,

And all the gracious order of the King

Within him has been broken and destroy'd.

So now the perfect leader and true King

Has pass'd, sore wounded, from his
thoughts' high throne,

And waits withdrawn where those who
drove him out

Can never reach. Perchance his golden
reign

Not yet has brighten'd our beloved earth,

But Angela is seeking for the King,
And late or soon the pure aspiring soul
Shall find her Eos in the inward world,
Whom evermore the outward world
    desires,
Yet evermore it wounds.

               O fair and sweet
The silken vesture of the outward world
Shimmers about the Grand Reality,
Veils and reveals it ever, with divine
Half-truths enchants us, yearning leads
    us on
To seek the soul within, yet evermore
Withholds the essence and the soul with-
    holds,
And dupes us with the dazzlement and
    dream !
Splendour of outward glory visible,
Grace of deft folds of drapery divine,
Elusive ever is your parable !

Deep, dread-sweet meaning lurks, we
    know, therein ;
That pageant's smallest particle may hold
The key to all ; but never bird has voiced,
Nor strong sea-music, nor the breeze or
    wind,
Nor any tone in all the world of tone ;
Nor the mute mystery of painted things
Hath pictured it. When shall we find
    it ? When
Discern the meaning written between the
    lines ?
Till then we love thee, world, thy lures
    allow ;
But when the soul is in thy beauty most
Profoundly steep'd, most then, she knows
    beyond
What point thy virtue loses all its force.
Thou art a satisfying, needed, great,
Consoling glory, but for us—for us—
Thou art not all-sufficient. Then away,

Sweet Mother Nature, if thou be not all
The soul seeks of the infinite, to her,
Sweet, thou art nothing ! Pageant, pass !
   And pass
All things which shew, set forth, or stand
   for that
Which is the one and ouly thing we
   need !
Pass, substitutes, how beautiful soe'er !
And come the signified, the beauty, truth,
We need thee, being part of thee, the
   whole !

Behold, the alchemist has master'd death,
And sets the cup of immortality
With its sharp edge of joy against our
   lips !
That draught is of scant service to the
   soul ;
Fate intervenes; we shall not drink
   thereof.

Take back thy gifts, great Hermes ! If
    our path
Lie straight through the strait gate of
    bitter death,
Through bitter death, needs must, we go
    to thee ;
Whatever price is ask'd we pay to reach ;
We must have thee.

            The grave is open now
Hard by the ancient church ; it is a morn
Of summer, and the bright sea, churn'd
    and soft
With a warm mist, low in the distance
    laughs
Amidst the pauses of the requiem.
The baffled seeker who had vanquish'd
    death
Goes down into the dread, cold, oozing
    earth
Amidst the gentle mockery of all

That gleams upon the shallow glass of
    things.

And Angela, sweet maiden Angela,

Even for thee the glad world wears no
    weeds !

Dissolved in tears too long, she weeps no
    more,

While humble villagers about her mourn

Her orphanhood, and one with deep-
    bow'd head

And hidden face, who long has loved the
    maid,

The thought-pale master of the village
    school,

Stands far away as his own hopes of love,

And hollow in his empty, aching heart

The death-chant utters a dull agony.

Is that the clod upon the coffin-lid

Which wakes an ominous echo in the
    bright

And genial air? We have all knock'd
    like that—

Ah, once at least knock'd at the tomb
    like that!—

And found it ever of all answering voice

Utterly void. Yes, we have knock'd.
    Perchance

The ghost of that which once we loved
    replied,

And that was void as any dust return'd,

Or crash of cold clay cast on senseless
    wood,

For there was neither truth nor meaning
    there.

So question we the grave or ghosts no
    more,

But seek we still the Great Reality,

And in the ripe and perfect time of God

The truth which never was in grave or
    ghost

Shall answer us.

Well, it is ended now ;

The highest quality of earthly hope,

The most magnificent of mortal aims,

Death swallow'd up in immortality,

Wealth inexhaustible and endless youth,

To see the spectacle of earthly things

Pass by and ever perish as they pass,

And to remain, the sole unshifting thing

Where all mutates, where all things else

    are vain,

And to partake with the eternal stars

" The glory of going on and still to

    be "—

All have gone down into the quiet grave,

And into nothing with the Alchemist

Softly dissolve.   Perforce we leave it

    there.

We know not why he labour'd all in

    vain,

We know not why the secret died with

    him ;

Perchance that liquor, had he lived to
　　drink it,
Because its ruddy mystery contain'd
Some thrice ten years of his poor life,
　　had proved
Sufficient to restore him what he spent,
And haply not.　Perchance the quest
　　itself
Did overreach God's possible.　We leave
Another problem in the hands of God,
Aud his kind, secret mystery of death—
Conceal it, Master, and do Thou lead on ;
Once we were quick to question and mis-
　　doubt,
Now we are weary of all questioning.
Shape Thou our course, we leave it all to
　　Thee ;
If we stand only in the night and wait,
We set the little issue of our lives
In Thy hands solely, stipulating nought ;
If day be fair or night be dark about us,

Safe in the harbour, out upon the sea,

Anywhere, anywhere, so Thou be by !

Yet, Master, purify the foul and dark

Within us ; make us fit to see Thy face,

And Thy great day come, and the King

　　return'd.

The rite is ended : *ite, missa est !*

O, may thy place be set in peace this day

And holy Zion thine abiding place !

While we go forth in faith with Angela,

Assured that God will one day judge the

　　world,

The great Accuser shall withdraw the

　　case,

And there shall none be guilty—no, not

　　one.

The weeping women of the house go up

With Angela once more to Mordred

　　House ;

The thought-pale teacher follows far
    away,
With sadder mien than ever mourner
    wore—
Over the hills and on to Mordred House—
Because the scant joy of his narrow life
Must somehow fructify, or wholly cease,
And he must speak with Angela, or die.
Peace, Destiny, be sure he shall not die !
Peace, froward Fate, his joy shall surely
    cease !
Behold them speaking in the garden now !
There is a tremor in the red, red rose—
He trembles ; the white lily is at peace
With Angela.   In perfect peace is she,
But see thou call not cold that heart
    which beats
So warmly in her for the whole world's
    weal :
Say passion never has the tranquil depths
Of her pure nature into ferment churn'd—

And why ?   The perfect passion of its
    heights

Has order'd all her nature unto God,

His Christ, His King.   Judge then—she
    does not look

From the proud height of silent snow-
    peak down

On the vexatious sea's disquietude

In some abyss which is the base of it,

And so with grace which is not gracious-
    ness

Make all words wither on the teacher's
    lips,

Till Paul's poor heart turns dead stone in
    his breast

Before the blank of loveless life to
    come.

She answers gently who has heard him
    well ;

Must chide her heart if e'er it turn'd
    from him,

Her childhood's playmate, ere her father
    went
To live in that old house upon the hill,
And in that feudal fastness follow up
His early quest of Nature's secret
    ways.
And since that time, if they had rarely
    met,
The sister's love she bore him had not
    fail'd,
A sister's pride she felt when tidings
    told
Of college progress and of prizes won
In open list.   But when he came again,
She knew not why, and took the village
    school
(Ah, to be near thee! cried the heart of
    Paul),
Abasing talent to a humblest scope
(Under thine eyes' light! sigh'd the
    heart of Paul),

And somehow grown to something more
   than youth,
The childhood seem'd to leave her as she
   look'd ;
And though with perfect love she loved
   him still,
The new time never unto her or him
Seem'd as the old dead days; then all
   her thought
For ever vigill'd by her father's toil
Till the great woe came, and the end
   to-day.
And now the sister's love was strong
   with her,
And wheresoever in the future time
God's will might lead her would his ways
   precede.
Then, pleading softly, she would have
   said : " Dear friend,
Bless me in taking all thy sister's heart ;
Ask not that heart a sister cannot give."

But, in among the lilies as she stood,

She broke in tears, whereat her gentle
voice

Dissolved away.   So stretch'd she forth
her hand,

As reaching out to one she could not see ;

And then, beholding how his hope began

To slip from him, to save it any way,

He put love by, and on another count

Would   strive   with   her,   urging   her
orphanhood,

Beseeching leave to guard her and pro-
tect ;

Was she not, like him, in the bleak, cold
world

Alone?   Was any who would shield her
there ?

Then she, replying : " From a distant
town

My father's sister writes of home and
love."

Whereat he urged her still, saying:
"You go,

And I shall never see your face again

Who would have toil'd and bled and died
for you.

God help me, my good angel goes with
you,

Which ever kept me since we kiss'd as
children

In all right ways and clean for you
alone!"

So, weeping still, upon her knees she
fell,

And cried: "My brother, do not press
me more!

You wring my heart. Now well indeed
I know

Your love has pass'd from love in
brotherhood,

But I can never be a wife to you,

And now am I more wretched in your
  woe,
Who live and suffer, than in my father's
  death,
Who is at peace with God, and com-
  forted.
Yet in a little while it may be well
Between us; God has call'd me, and I
  go;
And He will call thee at a proper time,
And thou wilt, too, be ready, and thou
  wilt go."

Thereat she rose, and very maidenlike
About him put the circle of her pure,
Warm arms, and held his heart against
  her face,
And kiss'd his cheek, and brush'd his
  tears away,
And bless'd and smiled and cried at him
  and fled.

But in the quiet chamber where she slept,

Again she knelt, and pray'd for peace in
  him,

Saying : " God, comfort him, and heal
  his hurt,

As I shall heal the sword-thrust of the
  King,

And give him also of the Holy Cup

In Arthur's day ! "

  The bright thought broke in light

About her lips and eyes ; she rose and set

The streaming glory of her glad gold
  hair

Behind her shoulders, then her mourning
  garb

Exchanged for samite white of broider'd
  robe,

Gold hemm'd and cinctured.   As a bride
  she stood,

And, wrought by inner ecstacy, raised up

Her pale, pure hands above her pale, pure
brow,

And look'd as praying saints, so utterly

Apart from earth that scarce her dainty
feet

Touch'd the oak boards, but rather poised
in air

She seemed, who in the middle heaven of
thought

Broke forth inspired, as the sky-seeking
bird

Amid the clouds shrilling sweet melody :

"My stricken husband waits me far
away—

My king awaits me, and I go to him!

I go to heal, I go to lead him forth,

And I shall come back to the world with
him,

Back from the dim dream-regions far
away.

" My royal husband draws me far away,

Who is the wedded master of my soul.

Sweet earth, farewell ; his magnet draws

    and draws.

I loved him, I have lived for him, I seek,

I know that I shall find him far away.

" Christ-cup amidst the mountains far

    away,

And blessed isle where paiu itself is peace,

All things of earth seem further now

    than you ;

Fleet is the dove when she has found her

    wings ;

For swift dove wings ye are not far

    away."

The little window looks upon the East,

And far beneath the scented garden

    ground

Exhales its fragrance, as the lonely man,

From his poor books, from the poor
   village school,

And from the squalid ring of vacant
   faces,

Looks o'er the meadow where the school
   is built,

And sees the hill which leads to Mordred
   House,

And sees the house upon the hill's bleak
   top,

And all his love, and life, and happiness

Go up, like incense from a garden ground,

To her who dwells on more exalted
   height

Than ever house was wrought on. Well-
   aday,

When she is gone the flowers will pine
   and die!

Will he, too, die when the rose light she
   makes

Goes back into some undream'd heaven
  of God
Where those who know not death in Him
  dissolve?
He thinks he will not die; he sees his life
All grey and cold as any winter mist,
And beyond what he sees more mist and
  grey.
He hungers for the love which will not
  come,
He thirsts for the sweet love which is
  not his;
He is an earnest man, whom thought and
  books
Have somewhat lifted o'er the common
  crowd,
And his expanded heart is capable
Of more than common love and misery.
The Great Dispenser meets him misery—
So is he wretched through his nature's
  range,

And wretched more because his ache and
    pain
Are such a common trouble in a world
So sordid in its range of circumstance.
Let him be wretched—if his hopeless
    life
Hold anywhere by one despairing straw
Of vain hope scarce acknowledged to
    himself,
Let him be cut therefrom, and, when
    adrift,
If he can feel another pang thereat,
Let it be his ! Let the steel enter in !
Let it drive deep ! Why should his heart
    be spared ?
Perhaps his heart will harden, and his
    soul
Will wither, like a dry stick in the heat;
Perhaps a time will come when Angela,
Her own dear self, could never melt the
    one

Or vivify the other.   What of that ?

Such wretchedness is old as any sin.

No doubt the man is earnest, true, and
  good,

No doubt that love, our life, would make
  him great.

We know not what he might achieve if
  loved,

For lesser men than he have wrought the
  world

Spans nearer up to God and the world's
  end

Whom love has wrought upon with
  mastery.

And what of that ?   God needs not any
  man,

Who any fashion can his ends fulfil.

Then let him harden, desiccate, and die.

He is not meet for Angela, the queen

Of all high thought, and mistress of white
  worlds

Within the mind which he has never
   glimpsed.

She is a mate for Arthur or a god ;
So let him hold his narrow nature bless'd
If he be given, when the King returns,
The scullion in the kitchen of the King ;
Aud if he die this night—long live the
   King !

The dun night settles on the dun dread
   sea,
The black night deepens on the wolfish
   sea,
The wind about the schoolhouse moans
   and craves,
The waste without is like the want
   within,
The want within is like the waste with-
   out,
And both are cold, and horrible, and both
Lonely and longing to be comforted.

I

There is no crumb of comfort anywhere.

The master sits amidst his books alone;

His love has read all meaning out of
 books,

It takes the life and peace from all his
 thoughts;

There is no purpose left him to pursue;

There is no hope or light from anywhere.

Yes, one star stills the trouble of the sea,

One rising moon puts out the dark of
 things.

Who is that knocking at the door so
 late?

O, lonely teacher, open wide the door!

It is the heart He knocks at; open wide;

Let Him come in; let Him sit down with
 thee,

Close by thy soul, and commune, commune there.

It is black, stormy midnight, and the
 lamp

Is dying utterly, the house contains

No oil; but is there none to help thee
  now?

Burst forth, bright moon, behind the
  melting cloud!

Ah, lonely man; ah, heart o'erwrought,
  not thou

Deserted!   It is Christ who sits with
  thee!

No soul deserted, Christ with thee, with
  all!

Come, Christ, in thy good time, and burst
  the bars

By which our arid natures in their griefs

Are so lock'd up from thee, so close
  withal!

The little window looks upon the East,

And far beneath the scented garden
  ground

Exhales its fragrance; it is wafted up—

The white magnolia sends a cloud of
  scent
Which oft in certain quarters of the
  wind
Pours tide-like through the casement.
  You detect
The faint, sweet perfume of white rose
  and red.
The lily languishes and droops and dies,
But cannot reach it.   Yet the maiden
  knows
Its virgin bloom is ever pouring out
Delicious life in aspiration there,
And it stands first of all her garden
  queens
In her pure love and vivifying care.

The little window looks upon the East,
The little table by the window stands,
The high-back'd chair is to the table
  drawn,

The maiden sits therein. It is deep
  night—

Deep night and silent—the beloved hills

Make a mysterious darkness far away

Against the phosphor splendour of the
  sky,

And the moon's marvel o'er the hill-tops
  comes

Full slowly. To the zenith she ascends,

And ever marshals round her shining track

The solemn pageant of all the starry
  heaven.

She dreams—the midnight's chill towards
  winter's cold

Lapses about her now. She dreams—
  the world

Is wet with dew. She dreams—the moon
  has set,

The mystic flush of morning fills the sky;

Birds in their nests stir, leaves upon the
  trees

Tingle and wake, life comes, sweet life,
    sweet morn.

She has dream'd well—she wakes—a
    rosy shaft

Of horizontal light, through hill-cleft, falls

Straight on her brow; it dazzles in her
    eyes,

It clothes her round, it slants upon the
    floor,

It pauses straight between her and the
    hills;

Her seems a pathway to the upland
    world

Expands before her. Is this waking now,

Or some dream-state, or something more
    than both?

She has not pass'd from out her gentle
    self,

But rather in her true self wholly
    merged,

Conscious of faculties and virtues new,

She rises up.   The antique masonry

Which rings the little window seems to

    melt—

She passes forth to find the Holy Grail

Along the pathway of the rising sun,

Along the red track, over the still earth,

Into the world of hills.   Assure her path,

Thou strong attraction of the upland

    places;

We who have seen them, we have felt

    thy spells;

Thou art the belt of some high mystery,

Which none can reach who toils with feet

    of flesh

To gain those summits.   We must pass

    like her

By aspiration's sudden rush to reach

That which thou hidest, the world's

    further side.

Attract us also ; we have long'd for thee !

It is not Gaul, Iberia, or Greece

We look to reach, but on thy further
  side
Another earth, another land and sea,
Perchance that country far hight the
  Soul's Home.

Oh, we have long'd for thee, sought thee
    through all ;
Sin has surprised us, our degree and state
Forgetting oft, but even in our sin,
Reaching towards bliss, ever wast thou
    our end,
Which art all bliss, thou true Home of
    the Soul !
Where is romance, where is there verse
    like thee ?
Poets, romancers, we, spell we our hearts
Ever with mysteries and melodies,
Thinking of thee, ever adream of thee.
Sweet is the world, gentle its ways are,
    bright

Its pageants, and our brothers of the
  earth
Are near and precious to our hearts.
  Take all—
Wealth, glory, love, although we cling
  to them,
Being all good—but take them ; and take
  us,
And shew at any price the Soul to us.
Ah, let us know the Soul, and God
  therein !
Ah, let God fill the dark and vacant space,
Which makes the vanity and void within
  us,
All and through all !   Yet bring us forth
  again,
Illuminate and saturate with God,
From out this Avalon, this ideal state,
In its subjective mode of private bliss,
Most beautiful, most dreamful, but for
  man

Unrealized till manifest without.

So may we ne'er find rest even in God

Till all our brethren rest in God through
us.

Where is the Christ we seek in this late
age?

We dare not say He stands upon the roof,

That is His light all sudden in the East,

Or comes He sailing over the western
main,

Nor yet that Christ is in the Hidden
Land.

We know that He lies dead beneath the
rock

Outside the city in the Holy Place

Till He is made alive in each of us.

Hail to the world of hills!—Aspiring
earth

At its best, whitest, utmost apex point,

Whatever is of transitory growth

Stripp'd off, till naked under heaven it
stands,

Heaven half attain'd. Ah, keen, trans-
lucent air !

Ah, cold, clear clusters, where the soul of
man,

Amidst a calmness of eternity,

Amidst a stedfast spiritual wind,

Enters in full possession of itself !

Ye govern the wide world which spreads
beneath

To yon most extreme bound which circles
all,

Which heaven alone enrings, and the
beyond

All merges into ether and the blue.

Even so the mind which dwells upon the
heights

Sways both the height and depth, commanding all,

Beholds all earthly things in heaven dis-
   solve,
And the eternal thought including all
Hold all the possibility of man
Within the circle of divinity.
Man is alone upon the hills with God ;
Man on the mountains of the mind abides
As one encircled by divinity.
Great is the sea, and the green world
   whereon
It washes is instinct with messages
Of vital moment; but the hills have high
And hidden secrets which are utter'd forth
There only. Sweet is every phase of life,
All human weakness sweet, but the strong
   man
Abiding fortified in lifted ways
Of highest thinking, puts the meaner man
Beneath him, enters in his greater self,
And so works upward towards the arche-
   type.

And on the hills the inspiration came

Which opens vision in the keen and pure.

As Moses, leader of his nation, saw,

In that same world, the mountain furze
    and wood

Alive all suddenly with mystic flame,

Beheld the Presence and the Shape Divine

So formulated from the infinite

That, as it seem'd, the fingers of a man,

Amid the leven and the burning bolts,

Wrote words of order and eternal law

On unhewn tablets of the mountain rock—

So ever Truth takes shape to lucid eyes

In sign and type, the formless form
    assumes,

And man himself seems but a woven veil

Which hides an inner wonder passing
    thought ;

When death that veil has rent, the light
    reveal'd

Shall star-like rise full grandly o'er the
    verge

And vast horizon of eternity.

Then if the splendid symbol of the Grail,

Amidst the azure altitudes of dream,

In the live light, in the red light, before

The burning glory of the solar disc,

Shone like a vivid circle of white fire

All in the morn, and all by unseen hands

Uplifted, though it was a type alone,

'Twas true, God wot, as any face we love

Which omens forth the love of God to

　　us ;

And Angela stretch'd forth her yearning

　　arms,

Standing tip-toe upon the crimson air,

But whether from the bless'd and holy cup

A magnet virtue drew the maiden on,

Or whether from her sweet white cistus

　　hands

(Which angel lovers might have kiss'd,

　　and so

Assumed new glory and fresh beatitude)

Some mystic force of soul-attraction
   brought
The wonder down, that wrapt one, lost
   in awe,
Knew nothing ; but it came, it brighten'd,
   paused
Above her head, and at her fingers' ends
A moment brooded ; in a moment more
She held the holy cup, she bow'd her head
Above it, till her gold hair in the sun
Stream'd over it, and through the veil
   thereof
Its darting rays possess'd all space with
   light,
Possess'd the world with fragrance, and
   a sound
Of canticles was voiced from all the chords
Which in the deep heart of created things
Are all creation's law and harmony.
She worshipp'd long, then reach'd with
   gentle lips

And kiss'd the rim.   Ah, witchery !
   Ah, love !
The sudden image of the face of Paul
Beneath her bent eyes shew'd a moment
   there.
It seem'd his lips, as she had kiss'd them
   once
In childhood, while the red wine in the cup
Throbb'd like that heart rejected left to
   earth.
It came, it pass'd, a haunting thought
   remain'd,
While in the ether of the mountain's crown,
The day's first lark sang love, and all at
   once
The chorus broke from hill to further hill,
For love possesses both the height and
   depth,
And reaching towards the infinite we find
Love there, as here, through all love,
   only love.

O infinite, eternal light of love,

Exalting all things in thy glory rare,

Our human beauty grows divine in thee.

Till in the vision of the world within

All types of beauty take the form of man,

And then, wherever we may pass in
    quest,

We still find man and love in God made
    one :

So may all love, from passion purely free,

With those we love pass on, and merge
    in thee, O God!

    *   *   *   *   *   *

Soft on the sea fell in the morning tide

Joy of the gold gleam, joy of the rose
    gleam, joy

Of virgin heaven's inviolate, laughing
    eye ;

Whereat the spuming, turbulent sea
    waves

Sank every one to ripples like a rill's,

                  K

And all the aureated ocean laugh'd,

Responding, with a bell-tone far and near,

And silvern cadences involved for ever

In their own echoes.   Then at once there
  rose

A vocal rapture o'er the teeming land ;

The breeze-swept pastures took inteuscr
  green,

The cornfields mellow'd to an August
  moon's

Red saffron gat from dream-magnificeuce,

The gilded upland's furrow'd earth put
  on

A plum-bloom vesture over violet,

And all the white-robed choir of mountains
  stood

Their snow-crowns' diamonds touch'd
  with Horeb light.

And once again up from both earth and
  sea

Amidst all festal notes a fragrance fill'd

The free, vibrating, lucent height of air
As light and happy as the lark therein.
So the descending mystery of the Grail
Diffused its blessings—peace of perfect
　　light,
Grace of all gracious odours, ministry
Of universal music, and the world
Was fed and rested. Such is Arthur's
　　day,
The preface to the coming of the Christ.
Ah, knightly vigil, to the end persist,
Over the morn and on to starry eve,
And yet again through visionary dark,
That so we may not miss the perfect end,
True dawn, true daystar, and true
　　plenitude !

That morn amid the marshes by the main
The confluential harmonies supreme
Centred about the hard-wrung heart of
　　Paul,

Who also felt that Arthur's day was nigh,

And half expectant towards the mountains
   look'd

Because perchance upon that central peak

Yon glitter's glory held the Holy Grail ;

Whereat the vision'd mystery declared

Amidst the altitudes to Angela

Shed sanctity and sweetness on his soul,

And when that gentle benediction pass'd

It left the soft light of a chasten'd hope,

As when tried hearts are comforted by
   prayer.

Then, all the marsh commanding, Mordred
   House

Uplifted in the summer glory drew

The teacher's eyes, a mile or more away,

But Angela seem'd close against his
   heart,

And close once seem'd her mouth against
   his lips.

BOOK IV.

THE KING'S COMING.

C OME, let us leave the earth! Forth
let us pass,
Upward aspire and rise, seeking the soul!
Here now is neither recompense nor peace
Till we have found the soul.   Peace shall
   be then—
A compensation full for common toil,
And a contented heart in little things,
Wherein our joy were mean till that be
   won
Which voids all littleness in life, and finds
The deep, magnalian mystery of God
As much behind the acorn as the oak,
As much within the emmet and the ant
As in the flying bird or soaring mind.

All other crowns save that which crowns
  the soul
Are but a bubble's lustre; nothing worth
Is any kinghood, if it lack the one
Eternal royalty which vests in soul.
But when the mind is royally therewith
Invested, verily the man is King,
Though he may scavenger in pauper garb
The king's highway.   Peace, let us pass
  in thought,
Ah, gently pass where all is thought in
  peace !
Let now the sinking sediment of sense
Settle in silence, and sublime above,
Potent and splendid spirit ! Prompts thee
  not
Pride in thy flight; thou art detach'd
  indeed
From things of earth ; thou hast thy way
  to cleave ;
There is a treasure aud a height to win—

Speed swiftly, who shall stay thee?
  Speed amain !
We know not where, but somewhere,
  somewhere far
Amidst the vistas and the violet,
Lone searcher of the pathway of the
  stars,
There looms the lucent kingdom of the
  mind,
Where is thy home, and where thy
  heritage !
Ascend, the city and the seat are thine,
And in the mystic courts and haunted
  halls
Learn the grand secret which our hearts
  are all
Burning to snatch. Yet when the light
  thereof
Enwraps thee, when its wisdom, master'd,
  makes
A vastness and magnificence within

Thy ravish'd nature, thou shalt surely
come
Back to the gentle and beloved earth,
From which no true mind ever took a
sure
And lofty flight but for the health and
wealth
Of that alone.   Come, let us leave thee,
Earth !
But wheresoever in the world within
The mind shall quest, its rest is all in
thee,
Till thou shalt rest in everlasting God.
Come, let us leave the earth !   Forth
let us pass.

Angela stood upon the mount alone,
Bearing the mystic chalice of her dream.
That was a high-uplifted place, most
keen
And mind-inspiring; far beneath her feet

The sweet world lay in the red light of
    morn

Like a rose garden ; from such heights of
    thought

The level highways of our daily life

Look fair of aspect ; 'tis proud thought,
    not high,

Contemns the common lessons of the clay.

O cherish earth, thy footstool, and the
    part

Thou hast therein, thou dreamer, that
    thy dreams

May be true gold !   Ascend, bring down
    the light !

Wherever thought may soar, here it re-
    turns,

And those who, upward striving, reach
    such height

As Angela's, know well their end is here,

And here the consummation of their toil.

So midst the adoration and the awe,

And in the ecstacy of light arcane,

While potent tides of spiritual strength

Through all her nature's open floodgates
　　pour'd,

An intuition of her quest's sole term

Inform'd her, as at times the sacred guest,

Received beneath the sacramental sign,

Will all the darkness of the heart and
　　mind

Enlighten　　suddenly　　with　　Godhead.
　　Paused

The lark in ether, paused the choric song

Creation litanied in light and joy,

And paused in dream upon the golden
　　stairs

The feet of starry angels, while she sang

So ever in the silence and the spell

May we pause also when the soul would
　　speak—

So also we when something, not our-
　　selves,

Which makes for more than righteous-
    ness, which makes
For very God in very inmost man
Abiding, all untraceably sets forth
The secret of the leader whom we need,
Till we know verily that leader lives,
And is not far from any walk in life,
Waiting to bend our nature towards the
    law :
The trembling light upon the golden
    stairs
Was hush'd into still glory, and she
    sang :—

" Speak, heart, and tell me where to find
    my lord !
While earth and sea keep silence, let the
    heart
Make answer from behind the bridal gift
Which in my hands I bring to heal my
    lord.

" The world is wounded like my soul's
    dear lord ;
O stricken world, thy master and my
    own,
Has never tarried far from thee or me!
I must return to thee to find my lord.

" I bear a bridal gift to bless my lord,
I bear a gift to bless thee, world, in him ;
Thy bitter pain shall end when he returns,
And my lord evermore shall be thy lord.

" O I have quested far to find my lord,
And now I know my lord is at thy gate!
He will not fail to heal and strengthen
    thee,
And evermore thy leader is my lord.

" So I return to earth and my great lord;
Receive me, earth, and love I bring with
    me :

Sing evermore, O wondrous main and
    shore,
And welcome in thy leader and my
    lord ! "

So from that sunkiss'd mountain's mystic
    height
The gentle maiden, like a shower of dew
After a dry and ardent August day—
So pure, so silent, and so life-bearing—
Descended, carrying the Holy Grail.
The companies of angels and of saints
On those bright stairs whereby the world
    below
Communicates with that which is above,
As shore with shore by tides that roll
    between,
With the harp-music of their wings
    possess'd
The upward path of bliss; from those
    bright walls

Which gird God's city, and from the
　　towers thereof,
The warders watch'd the maiden as she
　　went,
And far into the mortal mists and clouds
They mark'd the white light of the holy
　　cup,
Till once again the world which is not
　　dream
Closed round the dreaming soul of
　　Angela.

Fair are the mountain heights, keen is
　　the air,
Blithe is the soul upon the peaks of earth
Abiding ! Blessed are the high blue hills,
And bless'd the snow-bound, inaccessible,
Eternal Alpine crags and apices,
When on the highest platforms, far above
The line of ice, we stand, accomplish'd all
The human possibility of ascent,

While that which none can reach impends
    above,

And through the bleak East's shroud of
    pearl and grey

Widens a silent cleft, purple and vast,

Day on the mountains dawning blurr'd
    and red!

Yet from those mountains to the scented,
    soft,

Luxuriant plains, rich pastures wet with
    dew,

Exhaling ghostly mists beneath the moon,

Or in the noon, under the sky's white
    glare,

Wind-kiss'd and undulous and languor-
    steep'd,

The dreamer drawn by love of light
    divine

Seeks not in vain : him every phase of life

Illuminates ; prophetic are the woods

And forests, rivers revelations give,

Informs the humblest stream, the naked
    waste

Is haunted by strange voices of the soul,

And most, where'er it washes, the deep
    sea,

Sullen, monotonous, and multiple,

Interprets aye the mystery of God.

Then hail, old ocean! May thy strong,
    thy free,

Thy turbulent, unconquerable life

Increase within thee! May a soul be
    thine—

O, may some mighty soul, by God
    breathed in,

Inform thy vastness and thy voices fill

With still more varied meaning—every
    crest

Which spumes upon thee in this wind of
    May

Be some bright thought forth from thy
    nature's depth

By joy forced up to gem thy starry
    crown—
Be thy beatitude attain'd therein—
O grand and generous soul, the salt of
    earth !
May each white crest transport some
    joyful thought
From thine unfathomable nature's depth
To gem thy poet's crown !

                Homage to thee,
Because thy changeful nature never fails
To reproduce on earth the heaven above,
Bright type of that we long for ! Homage,
    too,
For constant earth on which our race
    abides
And waits the coming issues of the law.
Earth is another vesture of the One,
The One reveal'd in all, wherein we wait
The ultimate unveiling, and the Face.

                    L

Lo, now it comes, as morning slowly
    works
Towards doubtful eve! The space seems
    long betwixt
To us, my brothers; it is short to her
Who, bringing ministration to mankind,
From heights uplifted in the infinite,
Wots nothing of time's passage, and the
    lapse
Of vivid hopes with moments in the gulf
Whence nothing can be brought till God
    gives back
The past to His beatified, and makes
" Life's broken circle whole."

                    Another day
Has pass'd, and dim upon the water falls
The grateful silence of a windless eve;
It is too still for any star to shine,
There is a pale mist on the main and
    sky,

And the main spell-bound broods beneath
    the rocks,
And the sky spell-bound over earth and
    sea
Broods in the dewy hush. There are no
    sounds
In Mordred House : the spirit of the
    place
Is watching still, upon the West it sets
The old expectant patience of its eyes.
'Tis one day nearer now to Arthur's time,
And on such eve as this might Arthur
    come—
When all the world has lapsed so far
    towards peace
That sweet death seems to have released
    the world,
And it lies spiritual, pale, serene,
A gentle ghost, from all its labours free.
Ah, loving leader we have lack'd so long,
We are all ghosts of our best purposes

Till we can join with thee, so bright, so
    bold,

The inner spirit of the soul within,

The principle which binds our life with
    God,

The bond of brotherhood with Christ in
    God !

And thou art wounded and withdrawn
    and far :

Who hurt thee, Master, who hath stricken
    thee ?

All we have done it, as we dimly know,

Yet know not how, for in our foolish
    way

We love and yearn towards thee, our
    own best part :

While every day we live we hurt thee
    more,

And thou recedest day by day from us.

The mystic, weeping queens do bear thee
    far

In that strange barge along the waters
dim,

Or thy far Avalon, the moving isle,

Drifts further with thee over seas unknown,

While all our higher manhood goes with
thee.

Yet in another sense we feel thee near,

We know that none in truth has stricken
thee :

We have aim'd at thee madly in the dark

And pierced ourselves ; we bleed at every
pore,

But thou art whole ; thou art in very
strength

And lustre, and thou standest at the
gate ;

Thou would'st come in and take us to
thyself

And make us whole like thee. O open
wide !

What lets, my brothers? Is it lock'd?
   The key
Lost somewhere in the wilds through
   which we came,
Or wrench'd in battle from these van-
   quish'd hands?
Then break the senseless bars and let
   him in!
We cannot do it; they are fast, my
   friends.
Ah, pity, Master, come to us, come to
   us!
We cannot reach thee, open thou the
   gate!
He does not hear; to-day our need is
   deep,
It will be dread to-morrow, and he will
   come.

The house looks shrouded on the darkling
   hill,

The path is vague and dim which leads
    thereto,
The roads below upon the level lands
Are folded by thin vapours from the sea,
A broken byway passes Mordred Church,
And through rank meadows which the
    kine despise,
Amidst red weeds, up to the village school
Struggles with sad persistence, and is
    lost
Far in the melancholy miles of marsh
Which skirt the sad-voiced ocean in the
    West.

Be glory ever to the turbid sea
And that far-reaching marsh full oft
    explored
In many moods of visionary bliss
By gentle Angela !   May silent streams
Among the sedges and saturated grass
Their complex sinuosities pursue

And irrigate unseen the wide expanse

For ever !   May the bittern and the jay

Abide therein, the mournful plover call,

The plaintive sea-mew cry, the lark in

    spring

Sprinkle the crystal spaces of the air

With lucent dews of melody !   And thou,

The manifold in aspect and in voice,

Spread wide thy space, increase thy

    nature's depth,

And thy white-crested surges seen afar

Bleach in the wind and lift and multiply

In thy divine, immeasurable wrath

And in thy might for ever !   When the

    clouds

Disperse above thee in the central watch

Of the dread night, a thousand heavens

    of stars

Diffuse awhile tranquillity and light

On thy deep-breathing breast !   And joy

    be thine—

Joy in the revolution of the world,

In thy returning moon, auroral rays,

Sun's splendour, pageantry of evening
  red,

And the oracular vast of thine own voice

Which answers ever to itself, while earth

Shakes and is silent. The wind mocks
  thee not,

Which mocks at all things ; tempest
  wrecks not thee,

Because thou art a lone and awful being

Sublimed in tempest to the prophet's
  point,

Yet in the sunshine like a vestal soul

Still'd, fined, infused as with the peace of
  Christ.

From the high Eastern platforms of the
  earth,

From the steep mountains of the Morning
  Land,

Possess'd by vision, of the Grail possess'd,

The maid hath now descended, as it were,

Awaking out of her adoring trance

To find the golden chalice still enring'd

By spiritual splendour, to rejoice

Because she clasp'd it with her hands of
    flesh,

Because it was no vision of the night

But true, and with her in the world of
    old—

Beyond belief, bright, beautiful, and true !

Long hours unmark'd in that deep dream
    have pass'd ;

Years might have flown, the hour of all
    the dead

Might pulse upon the threshold, he be
    nigh

For whom we look, and Christ Himself at
    hand.

She stands at evening in the wilding
    path

Betwixt the village church and village
    school;
She knows that Mordred House is
    desolate
And cold and waiting. The church, too,
    is dark—
It is most lone and sorrowful and void.
The dead, expectant in their graves of
    God,
Lie sadly with the heavy earth above,
And still no angel comes to roll away
The stones, and no one to awaken them.
Ah, let us pity all the poor dead world!
Let us pray humbly for this world so
    dead;
To meet the doom divine by God decreed
Fill all our beings with nobility!
Perchance we shall escape unhappy sleep;
So may we rather wake and watch with
    Christ,
Prepared against His glory when it comes.

The mist about the dreaming maiden
    folds,
The night grows deeper round our
    Angela ;
There is a nimbus o'er the Holy Grail,
And in the light thereof, as she fares
    on,
All suddenly she sees the village school,
And that is also empty, dark, and void ;
The gentle heart of her most gentle
    breast
In pure compassion unto Paul goes out ;
The narrow door is open, and the house
Looks blank within, as all things bare
    of thee,
Oh, Love, are empty, and are dark, oh,
    Love !
I see thy hands uplifted, priest and King,
From thine anointed fingers pour in
    streams
A healing aura : whether late or soon

We do not know, but thou wilt come to
    us,

And nothing shall be sad that dwells
    without,

Or dark within; but we shall be like
    God

Forgiving all, because the world is full

Of pain and folly: none is wise but Love,

And that is God . . . . The house
    was dark without

And blank within, yet in such gloom
    perchance

He dwelt alone, and there was sorrowing.

She muses mildly iu her maiden soul,

And says: This sacred cup shall comfort
    him;

It cannot fail to heal and strengthen
    Love,

And on the other side of this poor place

God knows that I may chance on Avalon.

About the narrow corridors, within

Low ceiling'd rooms, the Holy Grail gave
    light,
And what it lighted in the humble place
That also it transfigured ; so it seem'd
That through the splendour of deserted
    halls
She traversed, up the stairways of a great
And royal palace, with that gift divine,
Ascended ghostlike.   Seeking as she
    went,
There seem'd a parable about her spelt,
And like that village school the village
    youth,
Its teacher, stood reveal'd, in outward
    mien
Lowly and little in the world's account,
But great within and full of mystery.
The Holy Grail made all things rare to
    her,
And love at work on Paul had grandeur'd
    him,

Who in the agony of wounded love
Found earth itself too little for emprize,
And from the barren flint of hopeless
    life
Had struck already with the spirit's steel
The fire of lofty purpose in the gloom :
So though the naked and unlitten world
It yet might pass electric, terrible,
Possessing being as a grand, strong thing,
Which if it did not beautify might yet
Inform.

      So spake the parable.   The maid,
With understanding mind accepting, saw
The vistas fill with glory, that pale youth
Whom thought, and haply something
    more than thought,
Had hallow'd slowly towards the beauti-
    ful,
Mounting the star-track of the infinite,
While the drawn nations follow'd from
    afar.

And then the thought of what the lad
    might prove
Did she but love him as he loved her,
    sent
The maid's blood flushing to the maid's
    pure brow,
And all at once the vision'd form of
    Paul,
Invested by the whole white light of
    love,
Shot up into the furthest heaven of stars,
Divine and dread. The sacred cup gave
    out
The fragrance of the purple grapes of
    God
Which in the Father's Kingdom, and
    upon
The old world walls of our dear Father's
    House,
Grow ripe and sweet against that day to
    come,

After the wine-press and the vintage-
time,
When at the supper-table of the Lord
We all shall quench the thirst of mortal
things,
And drink with Christ, the brother of our
hearts,
New wine, rich wine, eternal wine of life.
That vision paled. Again the Grail gave
light;
She knew the house was empty; with her
lips
Against that sacred cup, she pray'd for
Paul,
That he might never fail of any end,
However great, that God would gift him
for,
And might God gift him to eternity
And the eternal weal of all the world;
But ever and through all things God's
true grace

M

And all true love make glad and comfort
    him.

So through a narrow portal passing out

She found an aromatic garden fair,

Wherein a gate which on a generous
    mead

All in the moonlight gave. For, lo, the
    mist

Had lifted now, and, lo, the air was
    keen

And clear and cool, seem'd every purpose
    fair,

Assured and close, while all high dreams
    were true !

With open and illuminated mind,

From every doubt set free, in the scented
    time

Of silent dews and piping nightingales,

Amidst the magic and the mystery

Of moon-enchanted meadows and remote

All melancholy music of the main,

The white-robed maiden bore the Holy
    Grail.
Ah, never haply here in mortal life
Shall we who toil beneath the cross of sin
Bear that bless'd cup whereof she did not
    drink
For that her starry nature needed naught;
But would to God in this autumnal doubt
Where all that once was bloom is fallen
    leaf,
And all the woods wherein we worshipp'd
    once
Are wrapp'd in mist and drip with dreary
    rain
(There we invoke and nothing answers us,
But tempests scatter our poor holocausts,
The lightnings wreck our altars), would
    to God
We might awhile her virgin insight know,
Might see the end of all, as there she
    saw,

And taste the rest of the enlighten'd
   soul !
Return, thou clarity of sight and mind—
Expound the world ! Soul-Magic, weave
   thy spells !
Project the strength of the ecstatic mind —
Bid every gate unfold, all veils be rent,
All windows open'd ! . . . Inner Truth of
   Things,
The incandescence of thy secret light,
Made manifest to spiritual eyes,
Evolved its golden visions, vistas bright
Of scenic revelation ; and the maid
Drank wisdom in through all her faculties.
The mystic secret, unto God's elect
Alone reveal'd, in all things flash'd on
   her,
While night and wind were round her,
   stars and night,
While soaring upward, with no cloud
   involved—

O stellar, zenith-seeking sign of God!

Bright wax'd the orb'd moon-mistress of
the world.

So was she drawn, she knew not how nor
where,

But haunted ever by most holy thoughts,

And passing as she went from mortal
state

To something spiritual, strange, supreme,

A ghostly nature which from will to act

Did, void of effort or fatigue or pain,

Proceed with swift transition. . . Fell
the moon

And stately constellations sinking slowly

Behind the waters to the South went
down,

Till in a wondrous visionary way,

Beyond the meadows and beyond the
marsh,

And out upon a jutting point of rock,

As at the very end of all the earth,

In the first early saffron of the morn,
She, midst a magic hush of joy and awe,
Stood very pure and very maidenlike,
And the soft, small, caressing wavelets
    came,
Amidst a perfect stillness of the sea,
Up from that sweet, salt, splendid water-
    waste,
And sank with little melodies and chimes
All gently, gently, gently at her feet.

The early saffron turn'd a mystic gold,
As o'er the hill-tops, with a joyful shout
From all awaken'd Nature, rose the sun,
While like a parable of beauty there,
Stood Angela, the beautiful, the bless'd,
How still and stately in the morning
    light,
In the most royal light of that new day,
Which came so fair, so radiant, so peach-
    fresh,

That well indeed it might be Arthur's
    day,

Aud if the leader and the King we love

Should seem to tarry still, be still unseen,

For that his holy presence does not want

Invisibly about us.   It is here

And now, the impulse and the trust
    return,

The long-seal'd fount of fairy fantasy

O'erflows our soul once more, by life's
    dim deep

Long pausing, musing long.   No dream
    is dead,

We only slept and wake in dream again;

No golden hope is o'er, no faith hath
    fled;

The fortified intelligence within,

That virtue never in the past invoked

In vain from Nature, now collects her
    strength,

While benedictions from the world around

Shed down most sweet, most sacred influence.

It comes in dew, it comes at lapsing
night,

In Eastern flames and flashes, in the sea—

In the grey sheen of the full-breasted
sea—

Which breaks in ripples, crested, curling,
crisp,   .

Speaking great things—the mighty in-
flux comes.

Wind, darkness, distant, solitary downs,

Faint sky in morning reverie involved,

First lark, grand singer, in thy music's
cloud

Involved, invisible—and new-mown hay—

Their precious help vouchsafe!   The soul
is clothed

With priestly vestments; it is seal'd and
sign'd

With chrism of inspiration.

Is it thus

With you and me ?   Can it be thus, my
friends ?

The light illuminates, the transport fills,

The joy uplifts to very heaven of God

Us who have sinn'd and suffer'd, and
been shamed,

Us who are falling when we dream we
stand,

Who know not whether we are worthy
love

At our soul's best.   But she was pure
and fair,

And God's love girt her like a garment
round,

Poised where our senses at the height
would swim,

And being wholly clean and. void of stain

Was visited by suffering indeed

But fashion'd further unto sanctity.

What marvel then if in the morning light,

Beside the ocean's revelation, she

Pass'd onward through the dream of her
 desire,

As if the pavement of the waters smooth'd

To crystal stillness, while the Grail's
 white light

Encircled her, as ever sheeny cloud

Might fold the singing wonder of a lark,

And the wind's breath was full of balm
 and softness,

Even as God's grace breath'd in gift to
 man?

And so the mystic waters of the main

Were dared and cross'd, and so the sacred
 isle

Shone suddenly, and the stairway of the
 stars,

With Arthur face to face in Avalon;

So all the angel swords were beaten
 down,

So all the mists dissolving roll'd away;

But was it Arthur thus in mystic state,

O maid most sweet, amidst us here and
    now,

To whom the bridal gift, the healing cup,

The mystery of love of all the world,

Was by thee, white one, offer'd kneeling
    there ?

The glad hair all her sacred form enfold-
    ing

In wavy ripples to her feet went down,

And o'er her shoulders fell, on either side

Of that most glittering chalice, star-
    begemm'd,

Exhaling fragrance like a flower of light,

From her head's crown depended, as it
    hung

Was gently lifted outward by the wind,

So looking like the curtain and the crown

Above the altar when the monstrance
    rays

Gold sheen betwixt, the typal God within.

Her pure heart throbb'd behind it, and
   sent forth
Those dim and mystic chords of melody
Which in the hush of spiritual love,
Even on this bleak side of Avalon,
Do sometimes offer to the sense within
The secret of that island far withdrawn.
Where is the voice which shall in this
   late day
Shew forth the praises of the place of
   peace ?
When sacred love has taught it to the
   heart,
What tongue can utter that the heart has
   learn'd ?
It was the perfect peace of purest soul,
It was the region of the soul attain'd,
Where man alone shall rest, which thus in
   dream
Took outward shape about that spotless
   maid,

And, taking shape, obey'd sweet Nature's
    law,

And being close to Nature's inmost self,

Assumed the gentlest phase which Nature
    gives

To soothe and sanctify the outward
    world—

An amber softness in the solar ray,

A placid breadth upon the glassy stream,

Rich darkness in the verdure of the
    meads,

A languid curve about the upland slopes,

A wealth of woodland shade—but nothing
    strange—

No ghostly shapes which flitted through
    the gloom

In thickets ever from the light conceal'd,

No airy winnowing of unseen wings,

No bird or bloom unknown; and yet
    through all

The hush expectant hinting mystery,

The visible impress of a quietude

Which pointed pathways towards a deeper

    peace,

The graciousness which spoke of other

    grace,

And a mild music murmuring through all

Which seemed an overture by Nature

    made

Before the veil which is the bound of her.

The deep enchantment lulling outer sense

Awaken'd new activities within;

So sleep they not that dwell in Avalon,

Save as the saints do sleep who wake in

    God:

The heart and centre of the moving world

Is heart and centre of its euergy.

Ah, blessed place wherein the archetypes

Of all things here most perfect do abide

And actuate the types that we behold—

High thought, nobility, and rectitude,

And that transcendent love we call divine

Because devoted towards the perfect
    life—
That precious love which an eternal law
Gives ultimately back to human things
So to exalt them towards the archetype !

Thus, in the centre of that world of love
The virgin seeker found the love she
    sought,
As we shall also find our heart's own
    quest
At the true centre of the world within,
And whatsoever we have nobly dream'd
Consummately accomplish then and there.
But Angela had sought the perfect man,
That inner nature whom our outward life
Has long afflicted with such grievous
    hurt
That the true manhood no more strives
    with us,
But drawn apart awaits in kingly state

The coming of the far off healing time.

When shall a saviour of the age arise

To heal the leader's wounds?. . . . At
    least may we

Who cannot minister to man at large,

Except in lowly parable and song,

The individual King within ourselves

Make whole against the great day of the
    King,

And lead him forth with our own Angela,

Spirit and soul conjoin'd, and one hence-
    forth.

And so it seem'd the leader and the King,

Whom we have long'd for, in a lifted state

Of contemplation, as in waking dream,

Beheld the maiden and the cup beheld,

And, conscious of the old and unheal'd
    wound,

Stretch'd forth his kingly, venerable
    hands,

When of the healing draught she gave
    him free
And full libation; all about the seat
Whereon he waited for the call of God
The mystic mourning Queens that girt
    him round
Broke forth with one accord in strange
    sweet song,
While through their voices' ballad-music
    still
The heart of Angela, more subtly sweet,
Spoke from the inner world of melody,
And round that choric band the wide,
    wide world
Was manifest with mystic harmony.

So also, since the vision of the maid
Was passing slowly towards its perfect
    end,
And all earth's voices call'd on Angela,
Because the world, athirst from end to end,

N

Desired the healing draught, the Holy
  Grail,

The destin'd revelation follow'd on

Fulfilment of that mystic ministry.

In that same hour the heart of Angela

Vibrated with the great heart of the
  King,

And towards his throne the monarch
  raised the maid,

And the maid looking in his face beheld

And knew the King, yea, in that utmost
  isle

Of all the world, spoke his familiar name,

Not Arthur, but another, and still the
  King,

For love is King. So round about the
  throne

All music died, so all things round it
  changed,

The King was with her in the world we
  love,

And all the world in that same moment
    pass'd
Into the quiet mode of Avalon.

Now why King Arthur wore the face of
    Paul,
And why the cup sought out to heal the
    King
Was offer'd in the visionary world
To that pale youth aggrieved by wounded
    love,
Is haply one of love's deep mysteries.
O, unto us as to Saint Angela
It brings the profit of a secret law,
For haply we have left the world behind,
Renouncing also in our weaker way
All coarser ministries of sense and joy,
And quested after ideality !
So also we apart from human love
Have trembling enter'd in those upward
    paths

Where far away we glimpse the Love
   Divine,

Aspiring towards the Master of the Soul.

Now, she was pure by all her nature's
   law,

And meeter far than we to touch with
   God,

To unify with that which is within,

The mighty leader, the true spirit King.

But when within the visionary isle

She thus at length beheld him face to
   face,

'Twas human love that manifested there;

And so through man alone we reach to
   God ;

Who loves man best ranks nearest to
   divine—

A lesson for the leader and the king,

A lesson for the potentate and priest,

And most for those who, leaving earth
   behind,

To mystic heights, and that ecstatic bliss
Which comes in vision, from our human
    life
Would stand apart.

        O all ye sons of song,
Chorus of silver tongues speaking to earth,
True poem makers, if to one unknown
Ye list, forgive this maiden ecstacy
Which thus awhile forgets its parable—
Poets, forgive! What she, the maid I
    sing,
Intuitive, divined, I reach alone
By labour'd processes of conscious
    thought;
It dawn'd on her, a revelation sure,
But all in the sweet rose light of romance,
While round about the monarch's royal
    face,
And in the dusk light of his dreadmost
    eyes,

Rose light and gold light deepen'd
   solemnly

To purple's perfect splendour, type of
   love.

So royal love in that most holy light,

And virgin beauty's aspiration pure

Beheld each other in the peace and joy

Which is of Avalon. The world beyond

Pass'd from them like a troubled and
   moaning wind

Before the bright face of the arising sun,

And there was silence for a little space—

Sweet silence, sweeter lapse from conscious thought,

And down the tide of spiritual bliss

Floated the happy spirit of Angela.

   *   *   *   *   *   *

     *   *   *   *   *

From out deep vision, from illumined
   sleep,

The maid awoke, as she had waken'd oft ;

The little chamber from the world apart

Was filled with morning splendour, the
  free song

Of soaring larks, and all its floral scents.

What days had passed since Laban
  Mordred died,

Or unto earth his orphan'd daughter gave

Her father back, in such auroral light

As then ray'd out, such full swell of the
  sea,

She wot not, waking, nor what fever
  lapp'd

Her gentle limbs in langour.   Round
  about

That bed the women folk of Mordred
  House

Were gather'd, and the good old village
  priest,

With purple stole about his shoulders
  thrown,

Recited ever from his open book

In murmur'd monotone of mortified
Kind lips, *Ab omni malo libera*
Nos, Domine: A subitanea
Et improvisa morte libera
Nos, Domine—as dying in the dawn
She might have lain.   Suddenly then she
 knew
That some high seeming trance had
 steep'd her sense
In outward death, and, suddenly reveal'd,
Divinely bright above her waking eyes,
Bent down the dark, magnificent face of
 Paul.
She towards him lifting milk-white maiden
 arms
By that one gesture gave him love for
 love,
And all the world made music round his
 life
When such joy met him in the morning
 tide.

EPILOGUE.

SPIRIT of patience, spirit of faith and
    trust,
Look forth again from those dim win-
    dows' eyes
In haunted Mordred House. It is a morn
Of lotus melodies, of autumn sun's
Ambrosial mellowness and amber tints.
Wake in the woodland deeps, all blithe
    birds, wake!
Chime in the meadow world, all ye light
    streams!
Chorus of heaven's larks, on those wild
    wings
Soaring, entranced in light, through the
    long day
Sing ye, in ether lost, sing till the blue
Turns in the eventide purple and gold!

Sing till the hush of night heralds the
    stars !

Sing till the crescent moon brightens and
    sinks,

Falters and plunges and follows the
    sun !

Sing till the cradled sea rocks into rest—

Swelters and swirls in diaphanous sleep—

Lullaby, lullaby, sweet be the sleep !

Rye fields and wheat fields, undulous and
    ripe,

Strong for the sickle, for the harvest rich,

O multiply still more your golden ears,

And bow your bearded heads, and let the
    sun

Still further fructify your fair returns

To kine that plough'd and hands that
    sow'd in spring !

Here is a golden morn of Lyonnesse,

And here the day of Arthur and the
    King :

All hail, Lord Love ! Behold thy temple
    clean !

Strew'd roses scent it, and a thousand
    white

And vestal blooms, with folded baby buds,

Press'd by the passage of angelic feet,

Dispense their fragrance in the sacred
    fane,

Through nave and aisle, and wafted up
    to where

Thine altar looms. The lamps are lighted;
    now

The doves of young desire with censers
    stand

To sanctify the holocaust this day

That temple offers. There the mystæ
    stand,

And there the epopts of uplifted thought,

In circle drawn about a presence veil'd

And curtain'd in, where none but Love
    may come—

" Not Lancelot nor another," but the
  king.
Ah, golden gates and ivory towers which
  gird
The cedar citadel of maidenhood,
Fall down in music when his horns are
  blown,
And welcome, welcome, welcome in the
  king !
For evermore, alike at board and bed,
Until the sacrament of outward life
Shall pass away and shew the secret grace
Of inward being, to the bridal pair
More truly then than now in God made
  one.

And thus it fell upon a golden day
That Arthur enter'd into Lyonnesse,
More truly king than ever knight of old,
As Christ comes down and enters in the
  heart,

And then the void which aches and echoes
    there
Is straightway fill'd so full with light
    and joy
That all the human nature overflow'd
Assumes the likeness of divinity,
And makes about the peace-imparted soul
A nimbus whence, so long as Christ shall
    stay,
It sees the world transfigured. So he
    came,
A fair embodiment of human love,
Whereof whatever is of best in us
Is type and shadow, which through all
    these ills
Stills leads the race, still takes it slowly up
The starry track, and, howsoe'er remote,
In God's good time which never is too
    late,
Shall good and bad to our dear Father's
    feet

Most surely bring, all, all, in him made
　　pure.

O not with hosts uprisen from Avalon,
And not in ships over the western sea,
And not with banuers and emblazonments,
Nor manifested unto outward sense,
But felt and kuown and worshipp'd in
　　the heart—
Thus came—thus only comes—the Spirit
　　Prince !
So was it Arthur's day for Angela,
And when from out the visionary world
All men and women have their purest part
Of aspiration drawn to centre here
And beautify the race of which they are,
It shall be Arthur's day upon the earth,
While perfect human love as lord acclaim'd
Shall lightly lead us to the day of Christ.
And then, our Father, not in heaven
　　withdrawn,

As Arthur now in dreamful Avalon,

Long quested, seldom found, Thou shalt
be seen,

And lightly, Father, shall we pass to
Thee,

While the poor limits of our human part

Dissolve before Thee, and our meagre
wells

Of brackish love shall all be broken up,

And melt in music into Thy great sea !

Pass into Love Divine, pass, human love!

But from thy waters first deep shall we
drink,

That we may thirst the more, and quench
in God—

Quench all the thirst of life and end in God,

And then in Him be one with all we love.

So pause, O feeble song, and die before

The utter stillness of that silent sea

Wherein the small libations of ourselves

We pour, suspiring to be part thereof !

And thou, pure virgin, pass to purer wife,

And qualify through thy bright days to
come

To drink the chalice of the Mastery ;

It is not lost to thee, nor thy dear dream,

Which more and more henceforth in outward life

Fulfils itself, revealing also more

New lights uplifted in the world within,

Stars beyond stars, up through the path
of stars :

The light of Christ is on the mountains, lo,

Beyond the morning redness of the soul

The spirit's lustre sparkles from afar,

And overlighting all, Father above,

Thy glory manifests the infinite !

FINIS.

JAMES ELLIOTT AND CO. ;
TEMPLE CHAMBERS, FALCON COURT, FLEET STREET,
LONDON, E.C.